Scrapbooks of America™

Published by Tradition Books™ and distributed to the school and library market by The Child's World®

P.O. Box 326, Chanhassen, MN 55317-0326 ➤ 800/599-READ ➤ *http://www.childsworld.com*

Photo Credits: Cover: Front — Elio Ciol/Corbis, detail (right); Ame Hodalic/Corbis, detail (middle); Rykoff Collection /Corbis, (left); Back – Ame Hodalic/Corbis, detail; Richard Bailey/Corbis: 11 (inset); Burstein Collection/Corbis: 8; Elio Ciol/Corbis: 15; Ame Hodalic/Corbis: 7; Museum of History and Industry/Corbis: 16-17; Carl Purcell/Corbis: 29; Arthur Rothstein/Corbis: 24; Corbis: 9, 10-11, 12, 19, 20-21, 23, 30, 31, 33, 35, 37, 38 (top), 40; Stock Montage: 27, 38 (bottom)

An Editorial Directions book
Editors: E. Russell Primm and Lucia Raatma
Additional Writing: Lucia Raatma and Alice Flanagan/Flanagan Publishing Services
Photo Selector: Lucia Raatma
Photo Researcher: Alice Flanagan/Flanagan Publishing Services
Proofreader: Chad Rubel
Design: Kathleen Petelinsek/The Design Lab

Library of Congress Cataloging-in-Publication Data
Dell, Pamela.
  A song for Sung Li : a story of the 1906 San Francisco earthquake / by Pamela J. Dell.
    p. cm. — (Scrapbooks of America series)
Includes index.
Summary: Shortly before San Francisco's 1906 earthquake, a twelve-year-old orphan named Sung Li finds a box containing a locket with a photograph and an address, which lead her to a better life away from her demanding aunt and cousin.
  ISBN 1-59187-015-1 (library bound : alk. paper)
[1. Orphans—Fiction. 2. Chinese Americans—California—San Francisco—Fiction. 3. Earthquakes—California—San Francisco—Fiction. 4. San Francisco (Calif.)—History—20th century—Fiction.] I. Title.
  PZ7.D3845 So 2002
[Fic]—dc21   2002004766

Scrapbooks of America™

A SONG FOR SUNG LI

A STORY ABOUT THE SAN FRANCISCO EARTHQUAKE

by Pamela Dell

TRADITION BOOKS™
EXCELSIOR, MINNESOTA

Chinese artists used the same kinds of brushes for both painting and writing. These brushes were usually made of bamboo and animal hair.

Auntie Chow Fat burst in upon me, screeching like a maddened **peahen.**

"What are you doing now, you worthless child?!" she cried. Startled by her sudden entrance, I looked up and the bamboo brush fell from my fingers. A splatter of black ink smeared the small square of rice paper that was my canvas. My work was ruined.

Auntie Chow Fat saw immediately what I was up to. "Ah!" she growled. "Painting again? What did I tell you?"

Her eyes looked like two little black raisins pushed deep into the dough of her face, and her face had become the color of a crimson plum. I hung my head and said nothing.

Many consider **calligraphy** to be an extension of Chinese painting. During the 1200s, many artists accented their paintings with poems.

"What did I tell you?!" she repeated. "Look at me!"

I forced myself to meet her eyes. She grabbed my arm and pulled me roughly to my feet. "Answer me, you idle **sloth** of a girl!"

"You told me," I began, in a hushed voice of shame, "that if I don't behave, you will sell me to Fong Bo and I will be a butcher's slave."

"That's right!" Auntie Chow Fat snapped. Behind her, my cousin Chow Su had appeared. An evil smirk had settled upon her face. Watching her mother scold me was her greatest pleasure.

"Sung Li is going to be a butcher's slave," she **warbled,** her voice rising in sing-song tones, as if she were practicing her favorite tune.

My paint and brush offered my only joy while I was living with my aunt and cousin.

"Now you get in there and scrub every inch of that cooking room!" Auntie Chow Fat commanded. "Then you will accompany Chow Su on her shopping and carry her purchases home for her! Now go!"

Without a word, I left the tiny room that was my sleeping chamber in her house. They followed together behind me, two ever-watchful hawks making sure I did just as they commanded. But I had vowed not to stay much longer in that house. I would run away before I would be sent to any butcher. I would run away and become a fine painter and I would never have to see either one of them again. All of Chinatown would know my work. Perhaps even all of San Francisco itself. I would

8

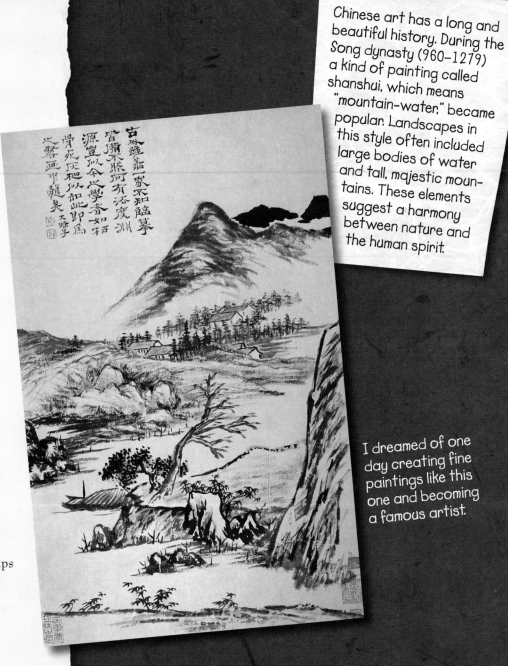

Chinese art has a long and beautiful history. During the Song dynasty (960-1279) a kind of painting called shanshui, which means "mountain-water," became popular. Landscapes in this style often included large bodies of water and tall, majestic mountains. These elements suggest a harmony between nature and the human spirit.

I dreamed of one day creating fine paintings like this one and becoming a famous artist.

From the tiny window in my auntie's home, I could see the busy streets of Chinatown below.

make my mother in Heaven proud of me. Everyone said she had great talent with the bamboo brush.

As if reading my thoughts, Auntie Chow Fat erupted into a familiar lecture. There was a hard and scornful edge to her voice.

"Just like your mother!" she hissed, from behind my back. "Just like she did, you think your beauty gives you the right to live idly while others work their fingers raw! Well, you are wrong, Missy! You live in this house and you will obey me. And if I catch you with that paintbrush one more time, you shall indeed go straight to the butcher. And I shall be all the richer for it, too!"

I made no reply, and she soon became tired of shouting at me. She and my cousin left me to my chores. For the next two hours, I scrubbed the iron cook stove and all the utensils. I polished the tiny window that looked down on the grocery stalls and spice shops of Spofford Alley. I rubbed the **teak-wood** chairs with oil until they gleamed. I scoured the wooden floor with a solution so harsh my hands turned red and raw and began to crack at the creases.

Just as I was finishing, Chow Su came to the door.

"Get up, Sung Li," she ordered. "We're going now."

"But I must change my—"

"You're not changing," Chow Su interrupted. "I'm ready to go now."

Her intention, I knew, was to shame me.

Between 1840 and 1900, approximately 2.4 million Chinese people left their homeland for America and other countries.

As Chow Su and I walked through Chinatown, we passed a number of merchants along the streets.

Incense burned throughout Chinatown, and I found the scent to be familiar and sweet.

My plain cotton pants and jacket were stained and dirty from the work, but she would make me go into the streets looking that way for all to see. As for her, she was stuffed into her own silk finery as if she were a short length of duck sausage.

⸺

The streets of Chinatown were bustling with early afternoon crowds. We passed a woman plucking geese in a poultry shop. Old men in the fish stalls nodded to us. The air was filled with a rich mixture of **incense,** smoked duck, and candied ginger. It was a lovely spring day, the nineteenth day of the third moon. In the English language, which I had learned some bits of, I knew the date

11

When I saw sisters walking together like this, I often longed for the family I did not have.

to be April 14, 1906, my twelfth year. Twelve years without the mother who brought me into this world, for she had died in giving birth to me. Six years later, my father and his brother, Chow Fat's husband, were killed on the same day in a terrible war between two powerful Chinatown clans. That was the tale the **elders** told, though I remembered none of it. I remembered only that I had spent the last six years serving my aunt and wondering about my mother.

Now I was serving Chow Su as well, though she was only three years older than I. As we came into the bustle of Montgomery Street, she turned her haughty head to me.

Many Chinese girls were brought to America with promises of nice lifestyles or marriages. But once here, these girls were often no more than slaves.

"Go to the **apothecary,**" she said, "and get me these things." She handed me a list of herbal potions written in her own crude script. "Then come back here immediately. Do not make me wait!" I turned to go and she entered into a shop that sold silk **brocade,** seed pearls, and ornaments carved from jade and ivory.

As I crossed the cobblestones, slippery with street **debris,** a flash of something in the gutter caught my eye. I stooped and pulled it from the **rubble,** wiped it clean on my pant leg. It was a small black **lacquer** box with a red silk tassel hanging from its clasp. Inside the box, lying on a bed of red silk, were a silver locket and a tiny piece of folded rice paper.

Quickly I slid my thumbnail along the edge of the locket. It opened like the wings of a butterfly to reveal a photograph inside. It was a photograph of a beautiful Chinese woman, her arm wrapped protectively around the shoulders of a girl about my own age. Both looked into the camera with the same serene eyes, the same delicate, serious mouths. A pang of loss struck my heart. I quickly closed the locket and returned it to the box with the rice paper. As no one seemed to be watching me, I slipped the box into my pocket and hurried to the apothecary. Soon I was back at the shop where I had left Chow Su.

I followed my cousin home, weighed down with her purchases. As we walked, I had time to think, for she did not speak to me at all except to warn me not to drop anything. Feeling the lacquer box thumping against my hip with every step made me wonder how such a precious item had come to lie in a Chinatown gutter. Currents of both curiosity and sadness coursed through my mind as I imagined these two fortunate ladies and realized that I would never own such a photograph of myself.

⌒

In the dead of night, when I was sure my auntie and my cousin were deep within their dreams at the other end of the house, I lit a candle. I pulled out the little black box from beneath my sleeping mat and again inspected the locket and the elegant photograph inside. I placed the box to the side and tried the

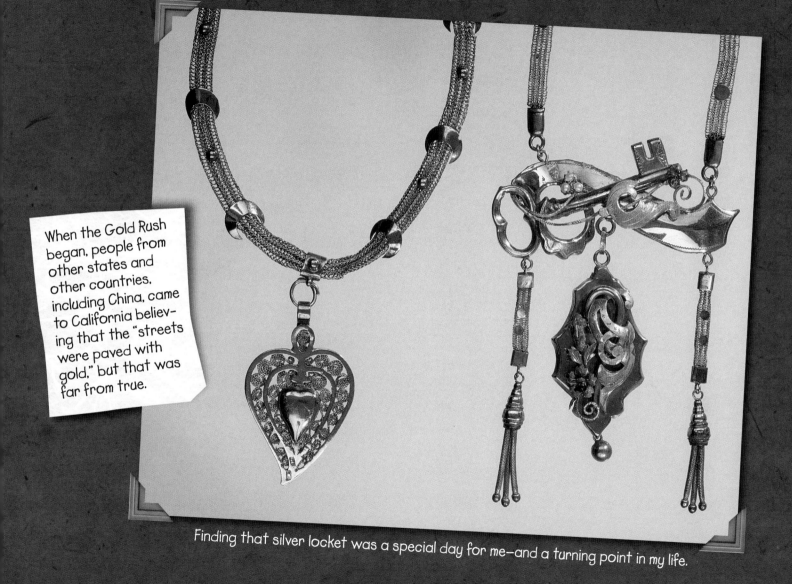

When the Gold Rush began, people from other states and other countries, including China, came to California believing that the "streets were paved with gold," but that was far from true.

Finding that silver locket was a special day for me—and a turning point in my life.

locket on. It hung from a silver chain, a cool
coin against my throat. Then I unfolded
the paper and read the Chinese characters
written there. It was an address in the city of
Oakland, which was across the bay. Next to
the address were the words, "Deliver Satur-
day." That very day.

I slipped the paper under my sleeping
mat. Then before I could unclasp the locket
and place it back in its box, the curtain
parted and there stood Chow Su, her eyes
narrowed in suspicion.

"What are you doing, Sung Li?" she
demanded. "Why are you up at this hour?
You have awakened me."

This could not be true, I knew, for I had
not made a sound. But before I was able to

Chinese Americans were known to be hard workers. Some people admired us for that, but others feared we would take away their jobs.

I knew that the owner of the locket lived somewhere in Oakland, across the bay where these men fished.

protest, she spied the lacquer box and rushed into the room.

"What is this?! And from where did you steal it?" She reached to grab it, but I beat her to it and wrapped my fist around it. She screamed and clawed at my fingers, trying to force them open.

"Give it to me!" Chow Su cried. She was stronger than I and pulled my fingers apart, snatched the box away. "You thief! You criminal! You shiftless child!" Her words echoed those I had heard out of the mouth of Auntie Chow Fat many times. And then all at once Auntie was there, too, and Chow Su was accusing me.

"That's it!" Auntie said, piercing me with her small mean eyes. "Tomorrow you go to the butcher! He will teach you obedience, and you will wish you had never defied me!" She grabbed my candle and put it out with one hiss of her foul breath, and then the two of them left me in darkness. I took the locket from around my neck and slipped it into the toe of my shoe, along with the little paper. Never would they discover that they had overlooked the finest part of my gutter treasure.

In the morning, Auntie Chow Fat forbade me to leave my room. She ordered me to get my things together, saying she would soon return. I did not own much. Only a tortoise shell comb, my bamboo brush, and a few pieces of clothing. I also had two most precious possessions, which Auntie had for some reason allowed me to keep. One was a carved **agate** inkwell that belonged to my mother and the other a beautiful fishnet of my father's. In the toe of my shoe, the smooth, cool touch of silver pressed against the sole of my foot.

I was still folding my things together when Auntie returned. I froze as she moved toward me.

"You filthy child! You have not even bothered to sweep the room?" She gripped my arm. "Never mind," she said. "Come! The butcher is waiting." With that, she began to hurry me toward the door, and I barely had

As more people from China made their homes in America, they created neighborhoods called Chinatown in a number of U.S. cities.

As Auntie Chow Fat marched me out of her home, I feared that I would soon be working for a butcher like this one.

a chance to grab my bundle. My stomach churned with a sick feeling, as if I had swallowed a cup of cooking oil.

Auntie Chow Fat hauled me past my **gloating** cousin, whose good-bye to me was no more than a joyful giggle. She dragged me down the dark, creaking stairwell to the street and into the bright light of early morning. But strangely, once outside we turned left down the street, though I knew the butcher's shop was to the right. Without a word, my auntie hurried me through the alleyways through the bustle of Stockton Street. All the street vendors and shoppers were too absorbed in their business of the day to pay any attention to the way she was rushing me along. We climbed the steep hill that is Sacramento Street and within a block, arrived at a five-story brick building with the street address of 920. There was a sign above the door that read, "The Occidental Board Mission Home for Chinese Girls." The hard thumping of my heart calmed a little, but I remained on guard. I still feared Auntie might be playing a cruel trick before sending me to the toad known as Butcher Fong.

Inside the orphanage, there seemed to

When my aunt and I walked up Sacramento Street, I had no idea where we were going.

In the late 1890s, San Francisco's Chinatown was a dangerous place ruled by fighting gangs called tongs.

be a great flurry of activity. I saw many girls like myself and also a few American women moving busily in and out of rooms. They were cleaning and polishing; it seemed all in preparation for some special event. I was left to sit in a large outer hallway while Auntie went behind closed doors with a woman who had introduced herself to me as Miss Cameron, the director of the home.

In a short while, Auntie emerged from the director's office. Her face was difficult to read. She looked like one of the stone dogs that guard the gates of a great temple.

"There!" she said under her breath as she approached me. "Be grateful, Missy, that your kind auntie has saved you from the clutches of Fong Bo. Here is where you shall live from now on. You are more fortunate than you know."

"But will you be coming to see me?" I asked as I stood and clutched my belongings to me.

"Don't expect it to be so," she replied in a harsh, low voice. I followed her to the door of the orphanage and hesitated as she opened it and stepped outside. She gave me a last look and smacked her hands together as if they were caked with something unpleasant. "I dust my hands of you for good. See how far your precious beauty shall get you now, you good-for-nothing child!" Then she slammed the door in my face and was gone.

None of the same blood flowed in our veins, but Auntie's daughter and I shared the

Some people in the United States called Chinese men "coolies." This term came from the Chinese words *koo*, which means "to rent" and *lee*, which means "muscle."

blood of our fathers. With them gone now, I had no family in the world. I stared out the window until I felt the gentle hands of Miss Cameron pull me away.

Bidding me to follow her, she took me upstairs and showed me where I was to sleep, among the strangers. All girls like me who had been abandoned, one way or another.

In a day or two, I decided this home for lost Chinese girls was not such a bad place, all things considered. There were friendly girls with tales to tell much worse than mine. Tales that made me shudder to think how close I had come to belonging to the butcher and knowing first-hand what they were

Once in the mission home, I joined the other girls who wished for real families, like this one.

The traditional religions and beliefs of China included Buddhism, Confucianism, and Taoism. But once in America, some Chinese people began to practice Christianity, the religion we were introduced to at the mission home.

Mission homes for Chinese orphans existed not only in San Francisco but throughout the world into the 1930s and 1940s.

talking about. Their terrible stories of being bought and sold from one master to another ignited a small spark of gratitude in my heart for Auntie Chow Fat. For all her hateful words, in the end she had spared me such a life of true misery. Like the other girls there, I had been rescued from a worse fate.

The third day at the home was Tuesday, April seventeenth. That day, I joined with the others in making final preparations for the orphanage's annual meeting. It was to be held the following day, with many visitors from far away. In the evening, the last touches were done, as fresh flowers were placed in vases and new curtains hung. I offered Miss Cameron the fishnet for decoration, and she exclaimed of its great beauty. Then she draped it in the chapel room, which made me proud.

That evening, we gathered together before bed and sang hymns in practice for the next day's performance at the meeting. I was only learning the songs myself but I felt that this "family," as Miss Cameron called it, was already becoming my own.

Each night, and that night was no different, I climbed the stairs to one of the dormitory rooms where the nearly sixty girls who lived there slept. I got into the bed that had been assigned to me and closed my eyes. After the lights were put out, I slid my hand under my pillow and pulled out a little cloth bag I had found to keep the silver locket in. I slipped the locket from the bag and clasped it around my neck. Each night, I slept with the image of the girl and her mother close to my heart, and every morning I returned it to the bag hidden beneath my pillow. I had already memorized the address where I believed them to live. I intended to deliver the locket there myself one day soon. That night, I fell into a peaceful sleep, hoping to dream of Oakland.

In the gray light of early dawn, I was awakened by a terrible shuddering. Jolted out of sleep, I felt that the whole building was being slammed back and forth by angry giant hands. More and more and more, the shaking grew, and a terrible roaring sound filled the room. The clock on the little stand near the window crashed to the floor, its hands telling the time to be 5:13 for evermore. The roar was monstrous now, as if some dark and hideous creature were rising up out of the earth to swallow us all in its huge, bloody jaws. I cried out and clutched tight to the metal bed frame.

"Earthquake!" someone screamed. It was a word that brought many more frantic cries into the air, girls calling out to each other and to Miss Cameron. The shuddering grew into a terrific jolting **spasm.** Mounds of **plaster** began to fall from above, and I feared we were all about to be buried under the creaking, cracking ceiling.

Beds slid in all directions, crashing into each other. Some girls had darted from their

We thought the earthquake was over, that morning of April 18, but there were 135 aftershocks that day.

The 1906 earthquake in San Francisco was headline news across the country.

beds, looking for safe places to hide. I heard the sounds of objects crashing to the floor, terrible thuds and breaking glass, creaking timbers. Beyond our room, the cries of babies could be heard now, too, like the voices of tiny frightened birds adding to the terrible rush of other noises. The terrifying roar, the horrific shuddering; all of it seemed unending. Then there came a deafening crash above our heads. The chimney had fallen onto the roof. Would we be buried in this rubble?

After what seemed forever, the roaring subsided, the quaking died away, and the house settled. But as we searched the house to see that everyone was all right, we also saw

More than 3,000 people died because of the earthquake and about 225,000 people were hurt.

that the entire place was in shambles. We helped the little ones to dress, and then Miss Cameron called us downstairs. We gathered in the kitchen at the little white tables, bowing our heads while Miss Cameron said a prayer of gratitude that none of us was hurt. Then we recited the Twenty-third Psalm from the book called the Bible, as we did each morning. For breakfast, we had warm bread that the matron, Miss Ferree, had managed to get at a bakery, and Mrs. Ng Poon Chew, a neighbor, came with hot tea and apples.

It was the last meal any of us would ever eat at the Mission Home. But before it was done, another severe shock sent us again into

After we survived the earthquake, we read the Twenty-third Psalm from the Bible, just like we did every day.

panic. We hurried with Miss Cameron to the windows on the east side of an upper floor and looked out. A thick column of smoke was rising into the new morning, as **ominous** as death itself. The city was burning in several places. I rushed to a north-facing window and looked out toward Spofford Alley and the rest of Chinatown, but there was barely anything standing. Most of what I could see was simply heaps of rubble. Seeing this, all the dread I had ever known in my life came back to lodge in my body.

There were tears, but no one complained when Miss Cameron instructed us to look around one last time before we abandoned the home. We had a long walk up steep hills

Even though the earthquake was over, fires burned throughout the city for days.

As we walked through the smoky, destroyed streets, we carried not only our sparse belongings but also a few babies who lived at the home with us. We tried to keep them safe as we journeyed toward shelter.

Chinatown was nearly leveled by the earthquake.

to get to the church where we would be staying for the night, but no one complained about that either.

As we walked to our shelter, carrying whatever we were able from the home, I fell in with Yuen Kum, an older girl. In a tearful voice, Yuen Kum told me that her marriage was only three days off. She told me that she was to marry a young man from Cleveland, Ohio, and how she feared he would never be able to find her now, or she him. When I replied that there was someone I needed to find, too, she asked me who it was.

"My mother," I said, staring at my shoes as we moved up the street over the rocks and rubble of the disaster.

⁓

The whole city was in flames. By Thursday night, our church had already fallen to fire, as had most of Chinatown, and we were in grave danger. Miss Cameron shepherded us to the docks, a tiring trek through many stinking, smoking blocks that had already burned. Finally we boarded a ferry and sailed north across the bay to a city called San Anselmo. There we were given shelter in the barn of a **monastery.** We learned too that we would remain there until it was safe to return to San Francisco and make a new home.

That first night, I could hear the flutter of bats' wings in the barn's high rafters. But with the locket around my neck, I felt strangely restful anyway. I dreamed of other homes: peaceful, safe, faraway homes.

⁓

We had been in San Anselmo nearly a week when Miss Cameron called me to her one morning. She was sitting under the shade of a tree, speaking with a man who was helping her make arrangements for our return to the city. I ran to her and in my hurry, the locket bounced from its hiding place inside my jacket. I had been wearing it since the night of the great disaster for fear of losing it otherwise.

"What have you got there, Sung Li?" Miss Cameron asked at once. She reached out to inspect it. "May I see?" I hesitated and

Though the earthquake's damage mostly affected San Francisco, it was felt from Los Angeles all the way to Coos Bay, Oregon, and as far east as central Nevada.

Fires continued to burn as we boarded ferries at the harbor and headed to the monastery.

then nodded. She opened the locket and stared at the picture of the beautiful girl and her warm and kind-looking mother. Lifting her eyes to mine, Miss Cameron asked me who they were.

It was impossible to hide from those eyes and so I confessed everything. All about finding the locket, about losing the lacquer box to Chow Su. About my wish to return the locket to its owner someday, even though the address I was looking for was so far across the bay in Oakland.

Miss Cameron gazed at me for a moment without saying anything, and then she asked me the address. I had said it so many times to myself that it slipped

San Francisco's City Hall cost $6,000,000 when it was built. It took only 60 seconds to collapse during the earthquake.

effortlessly from my tongue.

"Well," Miss Cameron replied quietly, "I have some business in Oakland myself. Perhaps we should call there together. Maybe . . . tomorrow?"

"Tomorrow?!" To me it was a magic word, and I burst out in agreement.

And so it was settled. The very next day, we set out for Oakland.

As we traveled over the churning waters of San Francisco Bay, I could see the burned and devastated city in the distance, still **smoldering.** It was now just a mass of dark destruction outlined against the sky. Here and there, I could see the bones of a building still standing. It was strange and frightening to see this view of the place I had lived since

As Miss Cameron and I traveled to Oakland, we could see San Francisco still suffering from the fires.

birth, a city where I had lost so much. I turned my mind to our destination instead.

At the door of a fine-looking old house in Oakland, on a street lined with shade trees, a Chinese housekeeper greeted Miss Cameron and me. In her kind voice, Miss Cameron asked to see the lady of the house. Only moments later, that lady appeared. I knew at once she was the woman in the photograph. And then the girl appeared, standing shyly behind her mother, but peeking at us with dark, curious eyes. Seeing them there together, I felt I knew them so well, though of course I did not know them at all.

Miss Cameron introduced herself as the director of the Occidental Mission Home for Chinese Girls and me as one of her wards.

"Sung Li has found something that may belong to you," she said then, and with that, we were immediately shown in. We were taken to a parlor with thick carpets and finely carved teakwood and lacquered furniture. It was the most beautiful and elegant room I had ever seen. The four of us sat together as tea was served.

Mrs. Wai Wu, for that turned out to be her name, looked at me with great kindness. Her daughter, Lily, appeared more curious than ever, but she said nothing. When our eyes met, though, a smile curved her lips.

"Well," said Mrs. Wai Wu, "what is it that has brought you to our home, Sung Li?"

I withdrew the little cloth bag from my

After the earthquake, many people took advantage of others' misfortune and began robbing homes and businesses. The mayor of San Francisco issued a "shoot to kill" order for these looters.

pocket and handed it to Mrs. Wai Wu. Lily watched as her mother emptied the locket into her palm.

"My goodness!" said Mrs. Wai Wu, looking up at me in surprise. "Wherever did you find it?!"

Once again I told my story, apologizing when I got to the part where Chow Su took the box from me.

"This is a miracle!" Mrs. Wai Wu exclaimed when I was done. "The jeweler was supposed to send his man from Chinatown to deliver it here days ago for Lily's birthday. We were told the man was careless and lost it. But now here it is!"

Mrs. Wai Wu draped the locket around

her daughter's neck and clasped it in back. Watching them, I felt a shadow of **mourning** shiver through my heart. The locket was Lily's now, not mine. Mrs. Wai Wu was her mother, not mine. But then Lily surprised me. She came over to me and wrapped her arms around my shoulders in a quick hug. It was as if I could feel her happiness spreading to me, and, for the moment, the shadow in my heart was forgotten.

"Well then, mission accomplished," Miss Cameron said crisply. She stood and looked at me. "Time for us to be going, Sung Li."

Before I had a chance to protest, Lily

When we visited Mrs. Wai Wu and Lily, we were served tea in elegant cups.

spoke for me.

"Can't she stay here with us for a while?" she asked, looking first at Miss Cameron and then pleadingly to her mother. "Please? For dinner, at least? Father must meet Sung Li, too."

Mrs. Wai Wu stood as well and put a gentle hand on my head. For some reason, it brought tears to my eyes.

"Would that be all right with you, Miss Cameron?" she asked. "We have been wishing for more children around this place, but Lily has been our only blessing in that way. Maybe we could get to know Sung Li a little better. Perhaps she could stay with us a while and see how she likes it here."

Miss Cameron hesitated. I knew she was **deliberating** over what to do with me. If I returned with her, I would sleep in a barn with sixty other orphans until our new living arrangements were settled. I already knew it pained her to have even one of us living under such conditions.

"Yes! Yes!" Lily cried, clapping her hands and looking at me to see if I approved. And of course I did. "A sister, Mama!" she added.

A blush of deep pleasure swept across my face, and I had to look away from them all to hide it. I thought of my bamboo brush and my agate inkwell, and of how much I should like to make a painting of Lily sitting

Even in Oakland, the earthquake wreaked havoc. The dust and ash in the air caused many people to get sick, mostly from tuberculosis.

The Wai Wu home had beautiful lacquer furniture like this cabinet. It was the nicest house I had ever known.

The 1906 San Francisco earthquake devastated the city and left many people homeless. But, as bad as that day was, it proved to be a new beginning for me.

beneath the flowering tree in their front yard. It would be my finest painting yet.

Miss Cameron looked closely at me. "Would you like that, Sung Li?" she asked. I nodded with lowered eyes, barely hoping. And in the next moment, it was done. Arrangements were made to send over my few things, Miss Cameron promising to keep in close touch with me and with Mr. and Mrs. Wai Wu. She said she would allow me to stay a few days and she would check in to see how things were working out. Then she hugged me and was gone.

I stood in the doorway with Mrs. Wai Wu and Lily, and we watched Miss Cameron walk down the wide steps to the street. At the curb she turned and waved to us, a smile lighting her pretty face. We all waved back.

Then Mrs. Wai Wu turned to me. Her face was a mystery, filled with all kinds of things. She looked sad and hopeful and joyously happy all at once.

"Welcome, Little Daughter," she said softly. "May this be the beginning of many blessings for you."

"Yes!" Lily agreed, a smile of great excitement lighting her face. "Come with me, Sister. I want to show you my room. I want to show you *our* room."

Their words in my ears seemed like a song. The most beautiful song I had ever heard.

THE HISTORY OF CHINATOWN DURING THE EARLY 1900s

Sung Li faced many hardships as an orphan in San Francisco's Chinatown in the 1900s. The tragic earthquake of 1906 had destroyed everything she called home.

At the time, there were about 25,000 Chinese living in crowded buildings within a twelve-square-block area. The first Chinese to settle there in the 1840s called the neighborhood "Little Canton" after an important city in China. But in 1853, newspaper reporters began referring to it as "Chinatown," and that is the name we still use today

The Chinese began coming to the United States in 1849 to mine gold in the California mountains. When gold sources dried up, many Chinese workers found jobs building railroads. Others opened their own businesses. Many

Chinese settled in the San Francisco Bay area close to one another. Eventually, this area became a successful tourist attraction. It was located in the center of town near the downtown shopping area and hotels. Tourists flocked to the fine Chinese restaurants, grocery stores, and special souvenir shops.

The Chinese suffered a terrible loss when the earthquake of 1906 destroyed about 520 blocks of San Francisco and most of Chinatown. Following the quake, fires broke out. The shock had overturned stoves and gas lamps, and it had broken electric wires. Gas mains had exploded. Firefighters could not put out the fires because the water mains had been damaged. For three days, fires raged throughout the city.

More than 3,000 people died in the earthquake and fire, and about 250,000 lost their homes. Fortunately, the people of San Francisco began to rebuild their communities immediately. Within three months, Chinese businessmen had plans underway for a new Chinatown. Because of their determination, Chinatown and other unique neighborhoods have been restored. They make up the backbone of San Francisco today.

GLOSSARY

agate a type of quartz that has layers of different colors

apothecary a shopkeeper who sells medicinal drugs and other items

brocade a heavy cloth with elaborate patterns woven into it

calligraphy the art of beautiful handwriting

debris small bits of dirt and rock

deliberating thinking carefully before making a decision

elders those in authority within a community

gloating enjoying the misfortune of others

incense a material that gives off a fragrant scent when burned; often used in religious ceremonies

lacquer a liquid used as a shiny coating for wood or metal

TIMELINE

1848 Gold is discovered at Sutter's Mill, California, marking the beginning of the California Gold Rush; large numbers of people from China, as well as from other countries and states, move to California to seek their fortune.

1860 San Francisco becomes the tenth largest city in the United States.

1869 The first transcontinental railroad is completed, in large part because of the labor of the Chinese who had come to make new lives in the United States.

1874 The Presbyterian Church founds the Occidental Board Mission Home for Chinese Girls, and Donaldina Cameron later becomes its director.

1882 The U.S. government passes the Chinese Exclusion Act, placing major restrictions on Chinese immigrants hoping to make their homes in America.

monastery a place where monks live and work together

mourning a feeling of grief or sorrow

ominous fateful, as though predicting disaster

peahen a large female peacock

plaster a hard covering for walls and ceilings

rubble rough, broken pieces of rock and stone

sloth a lazy person; name derived from a slow-moving animal

smoldering slow burning without flame

spasm a sudden, unusual movement or shaking

teakwood a hard, yellowish brown wood used in making ships and furniture

warbled sang with trills and varying notes

1900 Chinatown is quarantined during the bubonic plague scare, a tactic to make the Chinese appear dangerous or undesirable.

1906 On April 18, San Francisco is devastated by an earthquake as well as by subsequent fires.

1910 Angel Island is opened as a place to detain and question Chinese immigrants; it remains in operation until 1940.

1943 The Chinese Exclusion Act is repealed.

ACTIVITIES

Continuing the Story

(Writing Creatively)

Continue Sung Li's story. Elaborate on an event from her scrapbook or add your own

entries to the beginning or end of her journal. You might like to write about how Sung Li

became an orphan or what her life was like after the earthquake. You can also write your

own short story of historical fiction based on life in Chinatown before and after the San

Francisco earthquake.

Celebrating Your Heritage

(Discovering Family History)

Research your own family history. Discover if your family had any relatives living in

San Francisco's Chinatown or elsewhere in the city at the time of the earthquake. Ask

family members to write down what they remember hearing about the events of 1906

from older family members. Make copies of old photographs or drawings of keepsakes

from this time period.

Documenting History

(Exploring Community History)

Find out how or if your city or town was affected by the 1906 earthquake. Visit your library, historical society, museum, or local Web site for links to the event. What did the newspapers report? When, where, why, and how did your community take action? Who was involved? What was the result?

Preserving Memories

(Crafting)

Make a scrapbook about family life at the time of the San Francisco earthquake. Imagine what life was like for your ancestors or for Sung Li. Fill the pages with special events, family stories, interviews with relatives, letters, and drawings of family treasures. Add copies of newspaper clippings, photos, postcards, birth certificates, and historical records. Decorate the pages and the cover with family symbols or Chinese characters, Sung Li's silver locket, and drawings of San Francisco before or after the earthquake..

TO FIND OUT MORE

At the Library

Brimmer, Larry Dane. *Angel Island.*
Danbury, Conn.: Children's Press, 2001.

Chippendale, Lisa A. *The San Francisco Earthquake of 1906.*
Broomall, Pa.: Chelsea House, 2000.

Hoobler, Dorothy and Thomas. *The Chinese American Family Album.*
New York: Oxford University Press, 1998.

Stein, R. Conrad. *The California Gold Rush.*
Danbury, Conn.: Children's Press, 1995.

Wilson, Kate. *Earthquake! San Francisco, 1906.*
Austin, Tex.: Raintree/Steck-Vaughn, 1992.

On the Internet

Angel Island
http://www.angel-island.com/
To learn about the experiences of Chinese American immigrants

Eyewitness: The San Francisco Earthquake, 1906
http://www.ibiscom.com/sfeq.htm
For photos and descriptions of the earthquake

Museum of the City of San Francisco
http:www.sfmuseum.org/1906/06.html
For extensive background information, photos, firsthand
accounts of the earthquake, and much more

San Francisco Memoirs
http://www.sanfranciscomemoirs.com
To read first-person accounts of early San Francisco

On the Road

The San Francisco Museum and Historical Society
Light Court of City Hall
San Francisco, CA 94116
415/255-9400
To learn about the 1906 earthquake
as well as other San Francisco history

The Oakland Museum of California
1000 Oak Street
Oakland, CA 94607
510/238-2022
For more information about
Oakland and its history

ABOUT THE AUTHOR

Pamela Dell has worked as a writer in many different fields, but what she likes best is inventing characters and telling their stories. She has published fiction for both adults and kids, and in the last half of the 1990s helped found Purple Moon, an acclaimed interactive multimedia company that created CD-ROM games for girls. As writer and lead designer on Purple Moon's award-winning "Rockett" game series, Pamela created the character Rockett Movado and twenty-nine others, and wrote the scripts for each of the series' four episodic games. Purple Moon's Web site, which was based on these characters and their fictional world of Whistling Pines, went on to become one of the largest and most active online communities ever to exist on the Net. Pamela lives in Santa Monica, California, where her favorite fun is still writing fiction and creating cool interactive experiences.